From God, With Love

A Novella

OPHELIA LORRAINE

WESTBOW
PRESS®
A DIVISION OF THOMAS NELSON
& ZONDERVAN

Copyright © 2021 Ophelia Lorraine.

All rights reserved. No part of this book may be used or reproduced by any means, graphic, electronic, or mechanical, including photocopying, recording, taping or by any information storage retrieval system without the written permission of the author except in the case of brief quotations embodied in critical articles and reviews.

WestBow Press books may be ordered through booksellers or by contacting:

WestBow Press
A Division of Thomas Nelson & Zondervan
1663 Liberty Drive
Bloomington, IN 47403
www.westbowpress.com
844-714-3454

Because of the dynamic nature of the Internet, any web addresses or links contained in this book may have changed since publication and may no longer be valid. The views expressed in this work are solely those of the author and do not necessarily reflect the views of the publisher, and the publisher hereby disclaims any responsibility for them.

Any people depicted in stock imagery provided by Getty Images are models, and such images are being used for illustrative purposes only. Certain stock imagery © Getty Images.

Scripture quotations taken from The Holy Bible, New International Version® NIV® Copyright © 1973 1978 1984 2011 by Biblica, Inc. TM. Used by permission. All rights reserved worldwide.

ISBN: 978-1-6642-1860-4 (sc)
ISBN: 978-1-6642-1862-8 (hc)
ISBN: 978-1-6642-1861-1 (e)

Library of Congress Control Number: 2021900186

Print information available on the last page.

WestBow Press rev. date: 01/13/2021

This book is dedicated to all the
dreamers of the impossible.
Don't stop believing.

Contents

Prologue ix

A New Thing..1
That Tingly Feeling 7
And So It Begins..15
What May Be a First Date..23
Yep, It Was The First Date......................................33
This Day Couldn't Get Any Better..........................41
Thankful, Grateful Heart...49
A Little Tension Never Hurt Anyone 55
The Meaning of Family 65
There's Something In The Air 75
A Wonderful Gift 83

Prologue

"Listen to me, Cree, everything is gonna be okay."

"How do you know that daddy? How?" I asked my father as he lay there, breathing his last breaths.

"Because, baby, we know what's on the other side, don't we?"

He reaches for my face to wipe my tears but can barely raise his arm. It pains me to see him like this. I don't even know how a vibrant, healthy man in his sixties ends up here...like this.

"But what do I do without you? You're all I have." I put my head on his frail little lap and sobbed until I couldn't breathe.

"You have your mother and your sisters, sweetheart, and God—you won't ever be alone, baby." They were just outside knowing I'd want what may be my last time with him, alone.

What the doctors thought was one thing, turned out to be something they couldn't identify or treat in a short matter of months. My dad was rendered helpless by God only knows what, and all I can do is think of the moments in my life that he'll miss...that *we*'ll miss.

I know that he'll be in a better place once he leaves here but we didn't get to do all of the father-daughter things that little girls' dreams are made of. *God, please, spare my father. He didn't deserve this, God. God?* Silence.

"God, please!" I cry out but I hear nothing in return—and then I do. A loud, solid beep that is almost deafening. I raise my head and see a strange, almost peaceful look on my father's face. I was crying for so long that I didn't realize my father's hand had gone limp and I was in this room, all alone.

Hello, my name is Credence…

A New Thing

Okay, Cree, you can do this, I thought to myself as I walk down the long hallway towards the auditorium. This is where I chose to start attending this new church that I found. If I am being honest, I haven't set foot in a church in several months. My father recently died, and I was angry at God. He took the one person away from me who mattered the most. Not that God took him from me—it just feels that way, and it hurts, fiercely. It took me too long to realize that although my earthly father has died, I still have a heavenly one, which is why I am at this church.

I wade through the sea of people saying, "so glad you're here" and "welcome" and plant myself in a seat. The music is familiar and the sermon is awesome, so I decide that this was where I need to be. Once the service ended, the pastor invited any new people to a 'get to know us' meeting after church. I didn't have anything else to do, so I figure why not?

I grew up going to a very traditional Baptist church,

and I was never one to just *go* to church; I served as well. I mean, I was related to the pastor of the church I grew up in, so that was a factor, but I figured that I could go to this meeting today and maybe find a place to serve at this church. Serving people has always been the thing that helped me when I need encouragement, uplifting, or just a reason to smile.

I walk into the meeting not knowing a single person, but my extroverted personality gives me the confidence to introduce myself shamelessly.

"Hi, I'm Credence." I say to the woman leading the group, "Nice to meet you!"

"Hello, Credence, so nice to meet you." She says, giving me a big smile.

We converse for several minutes, then she rushes off to get some last-minute things together. I turn around and find a refreshment table full of snacks and candy. I grab a bag of wavy potato chips and a bottle of water and make my way to a table. Turning too quickly, I bump into a rather tall man and nearly drop my things. He grabs my elbow, catching me from falling.

"So sorry," I say, embarrassed, and continue on my way to find a seat.

"It's okay." He states, "I'm Frank—well, Franklin. But everyone calls me Frank."

I was in such a hurry to sit down that I almost missed

him speaking. But he's caught my attention long enough for me to see that he had the most beautifully round forest-green eyes. I have never seen eyes that color before on a brown man. They sure were gorgeous.

It takes me a second to recover, but I smile and reply, "I'm Cree, short for Credence, but everyone calls me Cree. Nice to meet you."

We make our way to separate tables and sit through the forty-five-minute meeting. It adjourns and I collect the remnants of my meal and take it to the garbage. I say goodbye to my table mates and head to the door. Before I cross the threshold, Frank stops me.

"Hey, Cree."

"Hi, Franklin?" I say questioningly. I am typically good with names and faces but right now I am just ready to go home.

"Right." He laughs. "I wanted to ask you how long you've been coming here. You seem so comfortable and familiar with everyone."

"Well, actually today was my first time coming. I have been looking for a new church for a while, then I found this one and decided to try it."

He smiles, "I did too. They post a lot of information and videos and I thought they were pretty cool, so I decided to check them out." He continues, "Do you live here in River Hill?"

"Yes, I live only a few minutes from here. I actually live close to every place I go, except work." My friends always tell me that I overshare, but I like to say that I am just authentically myself.

"Oh? Where do you work?" Franks asks

"At a communications company in Eastland, you?"

"I work at the college; I am one of the deans. And I live here too, south of town, though, so it takes me some time to get here"

"Oh, nice. It's beautiful down there." I reply awkwardly. River Hill is a beautiful and community-oriented town. Too big to be considered a small town but not big enough to be a city. The family that founded this town went the simple route when naming it because it literally has a river and a hill that separates our town from the two other towns that surround us. We have our own police, fire department, and hospital. There are a few elementary, middle, and high schools. We even have a college and apparently Frank works there.

We stood there talking for about ten minutes, which is unusual for me because I am not one who has long conversations with men. In fact, I've pretty much sworn off men until God leads me to the right one. I don't want to settle for someone I don't want or is less than I deserve just because the rest of the world says my standards are too high or that I need to make some compromises.

FROM GOD, WITH LOVE

I have been single for a while now and at first it wasn't a struggle. I had zero desire to be in a relationship, let alone waste my life getting to know a person only to be "too much" for him. I had seen too many relationships go badly in my family for those very reasons, plus infidelity and terrible communication. Even my own parents had divorced, remarried other people, and then divorced again; I just didn't think being in a relationship was worth the fight.

About five years into being single, also the same year I stopped counting, my perception of relationships changed—thanks in part to my best friend Dinah. She and her husband have such a beautifully amazing story that only God could have written it. Still, I didn't want to end up wasting my time, and the men that I have encountered either had no aspirations for themselves or weren't interested in thinking about the future. So, I decided on no men until God shows one to me.

Frank and I talk for a few minutes more, then begin walking to our cars.

"It was nice talking with you, Cree," he says as we reach the parking lot.

"Nice to talk with you too."

I arrive home and collapse onto my couch, thinking about my day. The sermon was on point for me. The pastor spoke about connectedness and how God made us to be in community with one another. I find myself in isolation these days, having lost my father, who I loved beyond words, and my best friend having recently moved across the country. Having an intimate circle of friends is something I have been desperate for but only began searching for a short while ago. Hopefully, my search ends here.

Then Frank pops into my mind. *Franklin. Such an old man's name but it somehow suits him. I just met the man, and I am already so fascinated by him.* I stop my thoughts from wandering any further. What in the world has come over me? One simple conversation with this man and I cannot stop thinking about him.

That Tingly Feeling

Weeks pass and I have found my routine at my new church. I like it here and have even begun serving. For as long as I can remember I have served in church, even as a kid, and since this is where I've chosen to stay, I also decided to find my place.

After church, I catch up with some new friends in the lobby and hang out to talk for a bit. Frank walks up, smiles, and greets us, then turns to me.

"Hey Cree. How are you?"

"Doing good, Franklin. Enjoyed service today, you?"

"Hanging in there, and it was awesome, wasn't it? How was your week?"

"So good. It feels the week just flew by, which is a good thing. Sometimes my work can be a bit tedious."

"I hear you. Meetings upon meetings all day, every day, does tend to get a bit redundant."

Our conversation continues this way for about fifteen minutes. We head to our cars and say our usual goodbyes.

This has become the routine for Frank and myself. We regularly talk for about fifteen minutes before *and* after church—we've done so every Sunday for the past month and a half. I have learned that he is from Louisiana, has one sister, and has only lived here for five years.

Frank turns back abruptly. "Oh, Cree!"

I look up from putting my purse in my car. "What's up?"

"Did you hear about the garden party that the Johnson's are hosting? They want to get to know people from church."

The Johnson's are a married couple new to the church.

"No, I hadn't. Sounds like it could be fun, when is it?"

"Later on, tonight. I'll see if I can get you on the invite."

"Oh, cool!" I say, a little too excitedly.

I get in my car and make the five-minute drive home. I drop my purse and keys on the couch and take out my phone. I text my best friend, Dinah, and tell her to call me when she gets out of church. I get out of church rather early, and she is in another time zone, so she gets out a bit later than I do. A short while later, I hear a *ding*. It's Frank letting me know the details of the party and that I am added to the invite. I thank him in reply and make lunch.

About an hour later my phone rings and I see that it is Dinah.

"Hey Di!"

"Hey yourself! How goes it?" She is such a silly one and I cherish her for it.

"It's going. How are you?"

"Pretty good. We had a guest pastor today. I guess we're trying out contemporary services." She attends a very traditional Baptist church. Which is funny, because I grew up in a traditional Baptist church and she grew up in a non-denominational church and now we've switched.

"That's funny." I chuckled. "How'd you like it?"

"Eh, could have been better. He did preach from the bible, though. So, there's that."

"There is that." I reply.

"So, what's up girlie. You texted me to call. Sounds important."

"I don't know, you tell me. Remember the guy at church I mentioned to you a while back? Franklin?"

"Yeah, the cute one with the green eyes that chats you up for half an hour every Sunday but still hasn't asked you out?"

I laughed. "Di, I did not say all that but, yeah. That's him."

"I'm just saying!" She laughs out loud.

"Well, some newer people at church are having a party tonight that I didn't hear about and Franklin invited me. Like, he literally made sure that I was added to the invite."

"Oh, wow. An interesting development."

"Not really, it didn't really seem like he was asking

me because he wanted to see me. It was more like he just wondered if I were going."

"Well that sounds the same to me" she replies. She is making sense, but I didn't want to read too much into it because frankly, the only way I'll know for sure is if he just flat out asks me on a date; though I am not entirely sure that he will. We chat a bit longer before ending the conversation.

A few hours later, I head over to the party. I made sure I brought my sweater because the evenings turn quite cool here at night in the fall. There are some people here that I recognize from church and some that I don't, but there is food and activities, so I think I'll be okay.

I greet my friends with hugs and take a walk around. The Johnson's live in the next town over from River Hill. A small country like place with lots of land and dirt roads everywhere. Their backyard is the size of two small lots and has a pool *and* a hot tub *and* a fire pit. I take a folding chair and plop down right in front of the fire to warm up. More people gather around the pit and one of them is Frank, who takes a seat right next to me.

"I see you made it."

I smile at him while he settles in comfortably, "I did, thanks for telling me about it."

"You know there's food, right? Over on the side lawn."

"I saw, but I'm not really hungry at the moment; I'll grab something a little later."

"Cool."

We sit in silence and watch the crackling fire light up the night. The Johnson's come over along with a few more people and we all sit around talking. I look over at Franklin and bravely start a conversation.

"So, Frank, you said before you were looking for another church and found this one. What church did you go to before?"

"It was Higher Ground. Closer to my side of town."

"Oh my goodness, really? I used to go to that church up until last year."

"Really? How long were you there?"

"Almost ten years."

"Oh, wow. Well, I was only there for a short time. I grew up Baptist, so it was different for me but honestly, I was just looking to find my place and grow my relationship with God more." He trails off then continues. "I mean, don't get me wrong, it served its purpose. Nothing is ever wasted, you know?"

"Oh I get that. I grew up Baptist too. I did love it there, though, and I met a lot of people who I still hang out with every now and again, and my relationship with God grew there as well. I guess God just concluded that it was time to leave." I sit back and stare at the fire some more.

"I think I'll grab something to eat now," I say.

"I think I will too."

We head up the grassy hill towards the side yard. As we are walking through the yard, and something occurs to me.

"You know, I had been at Higher Ground for a long time. I'm not sure how we haven't met before. I served all over the place in that church," I chuckled.

"I know, I was kind of thinking the same thing. Maybe we weren't supposed to meet yet," he says, almost jokingly.

"You know, you could be right." I never actually thought about it that way.

I smile as we continue to make our way to the tables of food. There is a large bowl of salad, pizza and hot dogs for the kids. I grab a slice of sausage and a water, and he grabs a big scoop of the salad and two slices of cheese. We then head back to the fire. After eating, we throw away our scraps then continue talking. Such a great conversationalist he is. He shares a lot of himself but also asks engaging questions. That is great for me because I love sharing. Talking like this with him felt very natural as opposed to how I normally feel about conversing with men. I was even comfortable enough to share my nerdy love of superhero movies and he didn't even flinch.

Several hours pass, and, having talked my head off with just about everyone there, I realize it is getting late and I need to head home. I look around and notice that Frank hasn't gone yet and he has a longer drive home than I do. I stop by where he and some others are sitting to say goodnight.

"Hey, guys, I'm heading out. Gotta get up early in the morning." I smile at Frank and tell him to have a good night. He stops me before I get going.

"Hey, you mind if I request you on social media?"

"Sure."

"Cool. See you at church then, yeah?"

"Yep!" I reply awkwardly. *What in the world is wrong with me?* I giggle to myself. That was so awkward. I guess this is what I get for disregarding men for so many years.

And So It Begins

The next day I woke up to a message from Frank. He has requested me as a friend but there is also something else written.

Hey there friend! I wanted to know if you heard about the fall festival in Eastland. It's gonna be superhero themed this year and I remembered you saying you love superhero movies. Anyway, just thought I'd share! Have a great week!

I smile and think to myself how awesome that was to wake up to. I get up, shower, and make a quick breakfast. After I start cooking, I take a moment and message Frank back.

Good morning! Thank you for this! I used to go to their festivals a long time ago, but I haven't been in a while. I may go this year since it is superhero themed.

A minute or so later, my phone vibrates—it's Frank, responding.

Oh, cool! I've never actually been. You wanna go?
Sure!

Great! I'll meet you there Saturday morning. I can't go on opening night I have late office hours on Friday.

Sounds like a plan! I say, chuckling at my ridiculous response.

Great! Have a great day! I hope it's smooth and goes by quickly.

You as well, thank you!

I eat my breakfast and get ready for work. I spent my whole day distracted by my early morning conversation with Frank. He is the sweetest guy and very much the opposite of every other guy I have ever met. I think I am beginning to like him.

After work, I spend some time with God, even longer than usual, because I have so much to talk to Him about. And by so much, I really mean Franklin. He is the kindest, most genuine man I have ever met, with the only exception being my father. His openness and intentional authenticity are incredibly attractive to me. I spent the whole week of devotions with God on the topic of Frank and praying the week would fly by so I could see him on Saturday.

When the weekend finally arrives, I am so nervous I call Di to have her talk me out of cancelling and to let her know that this is even happening, only now realizing that I never told her he finally asked me out; if that is even what this was.

Her phone rings in my ear one time and she picks up.

"'Sup?"

I laugh out loud, "Good grief! Where did that come from?"

"You know me, I'm silly!"

"I really do," I chuckle. "So, the party went well last week, and I really need your help."

"Well I figured it did, seeing as I didn't get a phone call."

"Sorry about that, but I left late and didn't think you'd be awake still. Anyway, Franklin invited me to the fall festival today and I am so nervous." I take a beat then continue, "We talked for nearly the whole night and long story short, he asked me to this festival today!"

"Well first of all," she explains, "you need to calm yourself down. Second, you have been waiting for this man to ask you out for over a month now, take a breather, girl!"

"Oh, I did that already," I giggle. "I need you to stop me from cancelling."

"Relax and remember that this is just a simple thing. You're going to a fair essentially and it is in the daytime *and* you're driving separate cars so if you absolutely needed to, you could leave." *Leave it to her to bring logic into the conversation.*

"You're right, girl. I can do this." I take a deep breath and exhale. "You're the best, you know that right?"

"I do," she replies.

I hang up and get appropriately dressed for a sunny, but still fall day and head to the festival. I pull into the lot and park but don't see that Frank has arrived yet, so I wait for him at the entrance. He arrives a short while later and meets me at the gate. We each pay for our tickets and make our way in.

I am more of a carnival game person and he is more of a ride person, so we take turns trading off doing one of each other's favorite things. We walk and talk. I get on a mini roller coaster called "The Amazing Slinger," or something like that, even though I am deathly afraid of them and he wins a couple of superhero plush dolls. One, he gives to me and the other, he keeps for himself.

"Ah, a closet nerd I see."

"You caught me." he laughs.

We continue this way until it gets late into the afternoon. I let him know that I had to run a couple of errands for the church and he understands. We walk back to our parked cars and share a silent moment.

"So. Weird handshake or awkward hug?" he asks.

"I think I'll go for the awkward hug," I laugh in response.

We hug, though not so awkwardly even though he is a good 10 inches taller than I am. "Have a great rest of your day! See you at church tomorrow."

"You too, see you then!"

I stop by the store on my way home for snacks and utensils for church tomorrow then over to the floral shop to get flowers for my dad's grave. I haven't visited him this week, so I decide to drop them off on my way home. I remove the dying flowers from the vase attached to his marble tombstone and place the new ones. I kiss my hand and tap my father's picture. "Daddy, you may have some competition." I chuckle to myself, get up, and head home.

The next day, Frank beats me to church, and I see him standing there talking to a mutual friend. I walk up and greet them both, with hugs. Our mutual friend walked away just then to greet someone else and Frank takes this opportunity to bring up yesterday.

"I had a lot of fun at the festival."

"So did I. I haven't had that much fun in a while."

"Really? There's a lot of fun things to do here, for a relatively small town."

"I know, right? I just need to be more intentional about it."

He smiles as if he's just had a brilliant idea. "You know, we're decorating for Thanksgiving weekend services next week and we could use more volunteers. Can I add you to the list?"

"Well, why not? I don't think I'll be doing anything."

"Great!" He exclaims, "The team and I have a recruiting bet." He laughs, immediately regretting it. "Just kidding, we're not competing or anything, but if we were, I'm winning."

"Hey, whatever you win, make sure you share."

"Will do."

Church was good and thought provoking as usual. When it was over, those of us that serve stay to help clean up. As I'm packing up the after-service meeting room, Frank and some others come in.

"You need some help?" Frank asks

"Yes, if someone could vacuum, that'd be great."

"Natural born leader, I see." Frank replies.

"Well, many hands make light work."

"So very true."

"Plus, teamwork makes the dream work!" someone says in another part of the room.

We all have a good laugh at that and soon the room is fully cleaned. Frank offers to take the cleaning supplies and put them back in their proper place. We say our goodbyes, and he leaves. I put the finishing touches on the room when I notice a cell phone still sitting on the table. I push a button on the side and the screen lights up; it's Frank's phone. I pick it and my purse up and head out the door. I look around to see if he is still at the church, but I don't see him.

I ask a few lingering helpers if they have seen him and one of them says he just took off. I decide to just take the phone to him. I mean, I genuinely would do this for anyone, but it did give me a chance to see more of him and his side of town. I go to the church offices and look up his address in the church database. Finding it, I head over to his house.

What May Be a First Date

The drive through his neighborhood is so beautiful with all the pastel-colored houses and perfectly manicured lawns. I arrive at his home and find it's a large, peachy color with white trim and tall palm trees around the edges of the yard. I walk up the steps to his front porch and ring the doorbell. It chimes a lovely grandfather clock-like song and within seconds, the door opens. He may have seen me drive up.

"Missing something?" I hold up the phone as the door swings inward.

"Oh, no! I literally just realized I didn't have it! Thank you, you didn't have to do this."

"I didn't mind, really. Besides, I was fairly sure you would be needing it."

"Yes, I will, thank you!"

"No worries. You have a beautiful home, by the way. I've never been to this neighborhood before."

"Well if you have time, I could give you a tour. It's a pretty big community."

It takes me no time at all to answer, "I'd like that."

I step in and wait for him as he grabs his keys. We go back outside, and he lets up the garage door with a button on his keyring. Inside, he has a golf cart, and not a small one with a couple of seats. His golf cart has a few rows of seats, and I am amazed.

"Let's tour in style." He smiles.

I get in the passenger seat next to him and we go driving around. This community is as large as he let on. In addition to the community center with the pool and lounge area, there was a place like a billiard room that sat on the banks of an exceptionally large lake. It was so beautiful out there in the open like that. Frank senses that I love being near the lake, so he stops.

"We can get out and walk if you want." He offers.

"Sure." I reply. "I love being near the water. No real reason other than the relaxing sounds the movements make."

"I'm with you there. There is just something about being in nature that makes me feel more connected with God."

"Yeah." I say, my voice trailing off. This is so nice, being here, walking around this lake. A strange feeling comes over me that I can't really identify other than it just feels good. I am smiling so big on the inside, all the while praying that Frank doesn't notice.

We lose track of time walking around the lake trading funny stories and life experiences. He is an avid sky diver and goes mountain biking, meanwhile the most adventurous thing I'd ever done was ride every roller coaster at Disneyland just to say I did, and I have never even been on a plane, let alone jumped out of one. Compared to him, I was kind of boring.

After a lengthy pause, I change the conversation.

"Can I ask you a question?"

"Go for it."

"Where'd you get your green eyes?"

He chuckles, "I was wondering when you were going to ask me that; everyone does. My mother is Swedish and black American, and my father is Haitian."

"So, your father's genes with your mother's features. Got it." I laugh.

"Yep. Now can I ask you something?"

"My hair, right?"

"I mean, there's a lot of it!" He laughs out loud. "Which parent did you get that from?"

"Completely my father. He was a *very* bushy man."

"That is hilarious!"

"Well, he was. I am not even kidding." I laugh, then go silent. "He died earlier this year."

"Oh, man. I'm sorry, I didn't know." He replies.

"Oh, no, you're fine. I was closer to him than my mom, is all. And I miss him."

"I am closer to my father, too. My sister is the mama's child; mostly because she's the baby."

"So, there's really only one sibling for you?"

"Yep, just me and her. You?"

"Middle of three, no brothers"

"Oh, wow. Your father was outnumbered, huh?" he laughs.

"For sure. He didn't mind, though."

"Can I ask you another question?"

"Sure."

"Credence..." he says slowly

"That wasn't really a question but, funny story. I was a bit of a surprise for my mom so right up until my birth, she had no name for me."

"How did she come up with Credence? It's a beautiful name."

"Thank you and it actually belongs to a friend of my mothers who happened to call her the day I was born. If it weren't for her, I would have left the hospital 'baby girl.'"

"Oh, no! For real?" He laughs out loud.

"Yep. Thank you Miss Credence, friend of my mom's, for calling her."

We continue walking around the lake, still laughing at

FROM GOD, WITH LOVE

my almost unfortunate name and talking. Before either of us realizes, two hours have passed. I suddenly remember I haven't eaten lunch and am beginning to get hungry. We make it back to his golf cart and take the long way back to his house, finishing the tour of his neighborhood.

I hop out and he thanks me again. "I really do appreciate you bringing me my phone. You're a lifesaver, Credence."

"Just Cree."

"Well, thank you, Cree."

After the impromptu tour of Frank's neighborhood, he invited me to a movie-on-the-yard event. It happened to be the same day that we decorated the church for Thanksgiving, so we essentially spent that whole day together. I found out that not only was he a closet nerd, but he also loved sci-fi movies as much as I do.

Since then, we've been spending time with each other very frequently. Mostly at church and community events but nonetheless, we had been hanging out with each other since late September early November. It's nearly Christmas now and we haven't really talked about what we are to each other, other than good friends. I know we'll eventually need to have the conversation, but I am not sure if I really want to acknowledge my feelings for him when I don't know what his are for me.

At church last week, Frank asked me to lunch on the upcoming weekend and said to plan on "doing something" afterwards. We agree to meet at a coffee shop close to his house that I am familiar with.

The day arrives and we show up at the same time. He opens the door for me, and I step through. I catch him glancing over at me as I search for a place for us to sit. "You know, I never figured you for a coffee-with-the heart-shaped foam person."

I giggle and respond, "You figured right. This place actually has the best herbal tea I've ever had, and their pastries are baked fresh every morning." I love this place because it's the perfect environment to just be. Large sun-catching windows, lounge seating, and a small room that has a bookshelf for guest's reading pleasure. Our server comes to the table and hands us our menus. After about a minute, Frank breaks the silence.

"You've been here plenty of times, you probably don't even need the menu."

"No, but I do look at it just in case I feel adventurous."

"So, then what would you recommend?"

"Well, I'm going to try one of their cranberry-raspberry muffins this time. I think it's one of the few pastries left for me to try. You should try one of their salads."

"Salad, really?"

"Yeah. They can pretty much take any sandwich on the menu and make it a salad."

He takes a few moments then orders an Italian BMT salad with a coke and I ordered my muffin with a three-fennel tea and honey in a separate dish. Our orders arrive shortly after and we begin to eat. I dunk my spoon in the honey then into my tea. I notice Frank staring.

"What?" I ask

"It's funny. How you put your tea in your honey."

"Oh, I'm weird. Dunking my whole spoon into the honey instead of scooping it is actually a functional thing because the honey infuses just the right amount into the tea and the spoon being metal helps absorb the heat, so it cools off quicker."

He laughs, "That was a fun little piece of information."

I shrug. "Well, what can I say? I'm quirky."

He smiles at me with his gorgeous pearly whites, "I love it."

I smile back and immediately turn my eyes away. We chit-chat for a bit more, finish our lunch and leave. When we get to our cars, Frank gives me a thoughtful look.

"Hey, why don't we take one car to the zoo today. You can leave your car at my house and we can ride together in my SUV."

"Oh, we're going to the zoo?" *I was wondering what we were going to do after lunch.* "That would be nice."

I am really starting to fall for this man. His relationship with God is most important to him, and that is incredible, but he is also generous, thoughtful, very intentional in his actions and with his words, and is genuinely kind. I still want to take it slow, though, and trust that the Lord is somehow leading this.

We get to his house, I park my car, and we get into his. The zoo is almost an hour's drive from here so it is going to be an interesting ride. This was a new experience for us, riding together. I am staring out the window, watching the trees zoom by, thinking about what this even means. I'm also thinking about my father.

Frank notices this and interrupts my silent reflection.

"What's on your mind?"

"I was just thinking about the last time my father took me to the zoo as a kid. He made up all these "facts" about the animals." I laughed thinking about it. "My favorite one was the one he made up about the cheetah."

I continue, "He said that cheetahs are called the fastest animal because they ate the competition, hence the name *chee-tah*." It must have been funnier than I thought because Frank threw his head back and belly laughed – hard.

"I'm here all night!" I shout wildly. *Nerd.*

Our ride to the zoo continued with us laughing the

whole time. We get to the zoo and walk around for a few hours, looking at the monkeys and the birds, passing by a rowdy bunch of college kids throwing grains at the alpacas until we finally stop by the Koi pond. By now it's almost sunset and the night air is getting chilly. I'm leaning over the fence lost in thought. Franks walks up and leans beside me.

"It's beautiful, isn't it?" He says, breaking the silence.

"It really is." And I wasn't just talking about the pond. I was also talking about this day I've just spent with him. It *was* a beautiful day and I think I'm falling in love with him, but does he see it? Does he feel the same way? *Sigh.* I hate not knowing.

After a moment he asks if I am ready to go. I say that I am, and we head back to his truck. The drive back to his house was serene as the sun set behind us. We arrive, and I get out and stand at my car door to unlock it. As I do, I feel Frank gently grab my arm. I turn around to see that he has a serious facial expression.

"I had a wonderful time, Cree. I really enjoyed our day together." He picks up my left hand and kisses it and I don't even know if I am breathing.

"Until next time, Franklin." I smile and wave goodbye, then head home—my stomach in knots and my head over thinking, as usual.

Yep, It Was The First Date

Instead of going straight home, I make a pit stop at the cemetery. If anyone could get me through this, it was my dad. I park, get out and walk over to his grave.

"Daddy, I really wish you were here right now. I met this man; his name is Franklin. I think you'd like him. He's smart and funny, and he treats me like a princess. He loves God as much, if not more, than I do but I don't know," my voice trails off. "We've been hanging out and I don't know what he's looking for out of this. Maybe I'm thinking too much, you know how I am."

I chuckled at my own words. My father always told me I analyze things to death and to stop overthinking and just trust my gut.

"I've fallen in love with this man who I've never even held hands with, let alone kissed, but we've been spending so much time together I want to believe he's falling in love with me too. I am trying to trust that this is God's doing and that I am waiting on his timing but man, this is hard. Daddy, I miss you."

Tears rolling down my face, I head back to my car and go home. When I finally do get home, I text Frank and let him know that I made it back safely. He texts back goodnight and that he will see me at church in the morning. I put my phone down then pick it right back up. I have to call Di and tell her all about today. The phone rings a few times before I hear her shriek.

"GIRL! I was wondering when you were gonna call me! I've been waiting forever!"

I burst out laughing, "Don't kill me, I just got home!"

"Oh, wow. That's like half the day, Credence." She is the only one that calls me my by my full first name, no matter how much I bug her about it.

"Well, most of it was with him but I did stop to see my dad afterwards."

"Oh, sweetie. Are you okay?" She has been so concerned about me since my father died. Just talking to her is comforting enough.

"Yeah, I am. Frank and I went to this coffee shop restaurant and to the zoo. It was such a wonderful day. We talked and talked and then talked some more," I laughed. "But the best part was when we got back to his house – because we took his truck to the zoo – he grabbed my hand and kissed it. It was so sweet and so romantic."

I pause, "Is that weird, though? That he kissed my hand even though we haven't really defined what we are?"

She takes a second to answer. "Not really. I mean, he clearly likes you and enjoys spending time with you..." I cut her off.

"But for all I know that's just as *friends* and I just don't want to think this is going somewhere and then be wrong. Dinah, I'm starting to fall in love with this man."

"Well, you know what I'm gonna say," she replies. "Have you talked to God about it?"

"I knew that's what you'd say," I chuckle. "At first, that's all I would do but now, not so much."

"Well if you want guidance on what to do, talk to God. Also, it's okay to ask Him for things. It's also okay to have feelings for a man, you know that, right?"

"I do, Di, but for one, I am afraid that I have chosen a man that hasn't chosen me as theirs and for two, I don't know for certain that this is even God's doing." I breathe a deep sigh.

"Sweetie," Di says, "talk to God, you know he has the answers you're looking for. And from my outside perspective, Frank is a good, godly man so it's not like God's gonna say *'I didn't choose this guy so get rid of him'*. Frank *adores* you, you do know that. So maybe work on accepting that for now. I'll be praying for you, my friend."

She says goodnight and is glad I at least had a good

time. I shower and climb into bed, staring up at the ceiling of my room, and begin talking to God.

God, your plans are greater than mine which is why I feel like I stepped into this thing with Franklin without your blessing and maybe that is why I am so afraid of what may or may not happen. I am falling for him and I don't know what to do. Should I tell him? Would that be unwise? As I lay in that thought, I suddenly felt the need to get up and open my bible. I land on Psalm thirty-seven, verse four.

"*Take delight in the Lord, and he will give you the desires of your heart.* I continue through verse six. *Commit your way to the Lord; trust in him and he will do this: He will make your righteous reward shine like the dawn...*" I stop there. "God will give you the desires of your heart." I recite out loud. I still struggle to believe this, most days, and especially now. I have fended off men for so long I did not even stop to think what I would do if or when a good one, the *right* one came along. I pray one final time to surrender my relationship, or whatever it is, with Frank to God and I go to asleep.

※

The next day, I awake and get ready for church. I arrive a bit early to hang out and talk with a few friends. I walk up and see that Frank is already in the foyer. He sees me and we greet each other with a hug. It felt different this time.

"How are you?" he asks.

"I'm doing good. How about yourself?"

"Doing great. I wanted to ask you something."

"Okay, shoot."

"Wanna go to the beach tonight?"

I laugh in response, "It's the middle of December, Franklin." *Granted, it does not get cold enough to snow here until about January, but it does get cold at night.*

"Right, that means we'll have the beach to ourselves."

I take a minute then give in. "Okay, I'm down."

"Good."

He smiles a big smile and grabs my hand, looping it into his arm. It takes me a bit to recover from shock given the unexpectedness of this moment. I mean, until now, no one at church even knew that we hung out outside of church events which explains the knowing stares that our friends are giving us right now. I thank God, for the very first time, that I am dark skinned so they cannot see me blushing.

After service, we stop off at the refreshment table and head out. He walks me to my car and hugs me.

"See you tonight?"

"Yes, tonight. At the beach. In the middle of December." I chuckle.

I get home, anxiously waiting for Di to get home from church to tell her my news. I change into some comfy clothes, make a quick lunch, and eat in silent contemplation, revisiting all that happened this weekend.

My cell rings—it's her.

"Hey! I was waiting to call *you*!" I answer.

"Well, we got out of church early and I wanted to give you a call before I make dinner. How was church?" she asks in a knowing manner.

"It was wonderful," I pause, then start again. "Franklin and I held hands." I sound like I'm in high school telling my best friend all the juicy details of my interaction with a guy. "Actually, he looped my arm into his as we were walking in church today and I nearly fainted."

"WHAT?!" So dramatic, she is, but I love it.

"Yep. After my initial shock, it actually felt kind of natural." I am smiling ear to ear.

"So, you're officially 'out' now."

"I guess. I mean, you know it's not something we've talked about but it's definitely a giant leap in the right direction."

"I'm happy for you. You deserve this, girlie." I can hear the excitement in her voice.

"But wait, there's more. We're going to the beach tonight."

"Oh, wow!" Again, with the dramatic.

FROM GOD, WITH LOVE

"I know, this is the first time we're going somewhere that's not so crowd oriented." I chuckle. I'm blushing just thinking about it. I don't know what exactly he has planned but it feels like the perfect night to talk about us.

Sensing my pause, she gives me some encouragement. "Girl, you've got this. Use wisdom and pray before you go. Also, just have fun!"

"I know and I will." My phone lights up in my hand. I check and see that it's Frank. "Hey, chica. I gotta go, it's Franklin. Thank you for being my bestie and walking with me through this. I love you forever."

"Love you too, sweetie! Have fun tonight and tell him I say hi!"

We hang up and I answer Frank. "Hey, stranger. How are you?"

"Doing pretty good." He replies. "So, I was thinking I could meet you at your house and pick you up for the beach. Does six sound good?"

"It does, I'll message you my address." I pause for a moment then ask, "Do I need to bring anything?"

"Nope. Just yourself, and maybe some of that humor from the zoo day."

I smile, "You got it. Oh, and before I forget, my best friend said to tell you hello."

"Well, tell her I say hey back. I'll have to meet her someday."

"Maybe you will one day."

I can feel him smiling through the phone. "Cool. I'll see you in a bit."

"See you then."

I hang up the phone and lay back on the couch. *Okay God, you see what is happening. Please give me wisdom and peace.* Almost immediately after I finished praying, I heard the words, "trust me." I have never audibly heard the voice of God, but I believe that I just had. *Okay, God, I am trusting you.* I set my alarm for five-fifteen to make sure I have enough time to get ready. I opted to forget the television and take a nap. I want to be well rested for my date tonight.

This Day Couldn't Get Any Better

My alarm goes off and I get up and take a shower. I tackle my hair next, brushing my afro back so that I can get my headband around it, then go to my closet. I am not one for having multiple articles of clothing. I quite literally have a few pairs of jeans, a hoard of fandom screen tees, a few dresses, and several jackets and cardigans.

I pick out a floor length sundress and cloth lined denim jacket. I put on a pair of leggings under it because it *is* chilly out and I find a matching set of earrings. By now it is ten till six, so I take one final look in the mirror. A few minutes later, I hear a knock at my door.

It's Frank.

"Hey, come in. I just have to grab my bag."

He just stands there staring. "You're beautiful," he says, and then walks in.

I lower my head, blushing. "Thank you, you look good yourself." He is wearing a long sleeve, gray checkered shirt with a hooded fleece jacket, dark wash jeans and sneakers. I have always loved when he wears this shirt.

"Was there traffic?" I ask him. I know there usually isn't much traffic on a Sunday evening, this is me making small talk.

"No, not really. Although I did get here quicker than I thought I would."

I lock my door as we step out and walk to his truck. He opens my door and I slide in. We'd get to the beach before the sun went all the way down allowing us time to watch it set. He seems nervous but then he reaches across the center console for my hand. *Just go with it,* I tell myself and oblige.

Before I know it, we are at the beach. He gets out and runs around to get my door; such a gentleman he is. I take his hand as I step out of the SUV. We walk, hand in hand, from the pier down to the sand; it's soft but easy to navigate. We walk the beach for a bit, silently, until Frank speaks up.

"You know, Cree, I asked you to the beach for a reason. I know we both love being near water so I thought that would make it easier to talk." I pause waiting anxiously for whatever he is about to say next.

"I feel like I haven't been fully open with you even though we have been hanging out for some time now." He pauses, this time stopping and facing me. Nervously, he continues. "I don't really know how to say this, so I'm just going to say it.

From the moment I saw you in the meeting after church that Sunday, I knew I had to get to know you. Something about you was just so inviting and I haven't felt this way about anyone in a really long time."

I take a deep breath as tears well up in my eyes and in his, the same.

"Franklin…" I start, but he stops me.

"Cree, I know it must have been difficult for you with me asking you out without *actually* asking you out and me not saying how I feel and that hasn't been fair to you. I know it has only been a few months but…" he looks down at the ground then back up at me, "I'm in love with you, Credence, I love you. I am so sorry for not even considering how you feel or even thinking about what…"

At this point, I stop him.

"Franklin, you have no idea how long I have been wanting to hear you say that or how long I have been waiting to say it to you." By now, tears are streaming down both of our faces, but I keep going. "You have had my heart from the moment you stopped me from falling that day. Because of you, I don't even remember why I gave up on finding love in the first place."

He leans down and kisses my wet cheek. I wrap my

arms around him, he wraps his around me, and we stand there as the sun goes down.

"I was so afraid that I was giving you mixed signals," he chuckles, breaking the silence. "I was hoping and praying that the timing was right, and I don't think I ever shut up talking to God about you."

I laughed. "I mean, you were at first, but I get it. I admit, I was a little confused and disappointed because I've felt like we completely fit together for a while now and I very intentionally haven't had feelings like this for a guy in years. Being with you is as easy as breathing, which is new for me, and it scared me a bit that you hadn't said anything."

"Honestly, I was afraid, too. For different reasons, but I was. I just know that I've needed to trust God to give me the right thing to say and do. I have monumentally messed these things up before and you are just too important to not give the best parts of me to."

We hold hands again and continue walking the beach. Now it's my turn to break the silence. "Can I be completely vulnerable with you for a moment?"

"Always." He replies.

"I asked God if I should tell you how I felt tonight. I have literally been talking to God about you since the day we met. All I have ever felt Him say is to trust Him and now I know why."

"Can I be completely vulnerable with you, now?" he asks.

"Always." I say, smiling.

"I've been in a lot of relationships. I mean *a lot*." He hesitates, then continues. "I always seemed to be with women who wanted me to be someone different, like who I was wasn't enough. Either I wasn't assertive enough or I was too needy. That seemed to be all women saw of me and honestly, I started to believe that I would ultimately end up alone."

"Well, if I can ask, what made you invite me to that party back in September? That was pretty assertive to me."

"Yeah," he says, laughing at himself. "I think I wanted to try to make up for what I supposedly wasn't giving enough of in other relationships. I realize now that makes no sense but at the time all I could think was I really want this woman to *see* me. I can't explain it except to say that I was just extremely attracted to you."

"Well, the only thing I'll ask of you is to just be you; the real you. I kind of like that guy." I nudged him and giggled like a little girl.

"So, what about you?"

"What about me?" I ask back.

"How were your previous relationships?"

"Well, I have only ever been in real two relationships. The first one ended mostly because we were both just too young and very immature. I didn't know how to define what I wanted and really just got into that relationship because I didn't like life at home."

I keep going. "The second one ended because I knew who I was and what I wanted but that was too much for him. He started using words like "clingy" and "desperate for attention" when really I just wanted to know that I mattered to him and how, on a basic level."

"Which is what scared you about me, isn't it?" he says, a bit concerned.

"Yes, it did, but only so much." I reassured him. "Even though you weren't *saying* anything, your actions were telling me that I mattered to you, and, up until the day we went to the zoo, that was all I needed.

After my last relationship I just kind of dated around, ultimately finding that I was not going to be okay with just being someone's date. Not that there's anything wrong with that, I just knew I wanted more than that and I deserved better. So, I intentionally stopped even looking. Then my father died, and I decided then I wasn't gonna start again."

"Well that's understandable." He says, sounding much less concerned. "I became a serial dater trying to prove to "the next one" that I was worth loving. With you I don't have to prove anything, and I am so grateful to have found you."

FROM GOD, WITH LOVE

We turn back and start walking back to the pier. As we get close to Frank's truck, he stops me. "Wait here," he says, as he runs up to the truck.

It takes him a minute, then I see him pull out a large blanket. Running back down, he unfolds it, and we sit. He wraps one side around him and the other side around me.

"I love you, Credence." He says as I lean into his shoulder

"I love you, Franklin."

Thank you, God.

Thankful, Grateful Heart

We sit and watch the sun completely disappear into the ocean before we decide to leave. Franklin stands then leans down and grabs my hand to help me up, smiling from ear to ear.

"What?" I ask him.

"I feel like a heavy weight's been lifted off of my shoulders, but I'm a little afraid that I might mess this up."

"Well, this is new for both of us so there is definitely a chance that we both could mess it up, but we shouldn't let that stop us, should we?"

"No. No, we shouldn't." He picks up the blanket, shakes the sand off and folds it up. I lean in for a kiss and he obliges. We walk back to his truck and take off. I am lost in thought the whole way back to my house. *I can't believe this is happening...to me. I'm not entirely sure I even deserve this, God.*

I am still inside my own head as we pull up to my

house. Frank taps my hand to get my attention. "Hey, you good?"

"I very much am." I respond. He gets out, comes to my side of the truck and opens my door, letting me out. "Whenever I meet your parents, remind me to tell them thank you."

"Thank you?"

"Yes, for raising such a gentleman."

"I'll do that," he chuckles. Now standing at my front door, we say our goodnights.

"No matter how this plays out, I will always be grateful for tonight." I say to him as I grab his hand and squeeze it.

"Me too." He replies.

We hug goodbye and he gets into his truck and waits until I am safely inside. I am still in awe that this has even happened while still trying to make sense of it. *My literal dream has come true and I don't know what or how to feel about it.*

I take out my cell to check the time as I start to relax on my couch. It's still early enough for me to call Di so I do. She answers on the first ring.

"You weren't waiting or anything?" I ask her.

"Oh, you best believe it! Give me every detail!"

"I need to be telling *you* to calm *yourself*!" I laugh in response. "But seriously, you were absolutely right. I definitely need to keep praying and trust that this wasn't some monumental joke from the universe."

"Girl, you know God has you. And I know from experience that it is easier said than done but it is completely worth it."

"I really know. It was the most surreal night, Di. First, he apologized for being so nondescript when asking me to go places with him. At first I thought he was maybe doing a man's version of playing it safe but then he started speaking openly and being vulnerable and told me why he was behaving the way he was. He still has issues from his past relationships, which is understandable."

"I mean, it isn't an excuse, but I am glad he apologized; that must have taken some courage on his part."

"It did and I am grateful to have found someone who can be vulnerable when he needs to be."

"Found someone?" she asks, intrigued. "So you think he is the one?" I can hear her I-told-you-so voice through the phone.

"Di, I really want to say that I have. I honestly believe he is but for some reason, I can't get it out of my mind that it should have been much harder than this. I mean, in the beginning, it *was* hard; you know, the waiting. And you know how I feel about that *the one* business." I laughed.

"I know and I definitely understand the difficulty in

the waiting. I guess my question is, then, do you feel he is the one for you?"

"Absolutely. He is everything I could have asked God for and more, but never in a million years imagined I'd ever have." I get chills replaying tonight in conversation with her. Not just the romance of it all but just at how much my fears have dissipated, knowing that I have found my person.

"I am so happy for you, sweetie. I could just tell the way you talk about how you two are with each other that you fit together." She pauses for a moment then keeps going. "You know your worth and you haven't settled for less than you deserve but also know that you don't always have to *deserve* good things; sometimes God gives us gifts just because we're his children."

"If I never understood that before, Dinah, I do now. I have thanked God profusely for Franklin and while I still haven't completely wrapped my head around it, I am satisfied remaining in the moment."

"This is so wonderful, Credence, and I am so excited to get to go through this with you."

"Same, friend, same." I reply, relieved to have her in my life. "Oh, and I didn't actually tell you the best part."

"Oh, there's more!" she says, excitedly.

"Yes." I laughed. "We walked the beach, holding hands, and talked about our feelings for each other. We also talked about what was going through each of our minds every time we went out; it was kind of funny."

Still chuckling to myself, I continue, "It was funny, some of the things he thought he would do to blow it with me and even funnier that we both were praying to God on what to do or say next."

"Two peas in a pod, you two." She says, now chuckling herself.

"The icing on the cake, though Dinah, he finally just says, *I love you, Credence*' and I was crying myself into a puddle."

"I bet! My goodness girl, so amazing and such a testament to your patience and God's love for you. Everything you waited on, cried, hoped and prayed for is becoming real. I am so proud of you!" After that, we were both in a puddle.

"Well, darling" she says, "I can't wait to see this incredible journey unfold. I love you and as usual, I'll be praying for you."

"Thank you, doll. Love you, too." I shower and get ready for bed but take a moment to just pray.

"God, I don't even know where to begin, except to just say, thank you. Thank you for Franklin and all that he is, for tonight, for giving us both the confidence to trust ourselves and You in what was probably the scariest times in our lives." I take a deep breath and continue.

OPHELIA LORRAINE

"I want to start believing in you in the way that I know I should but it's hard when bad things happen or when things I don't understand or expect happen. I definitely need your help in this area but now I think I'm going to actively try. I don't want to be mad at you anymore, God, I just don't." *I'm positive that God thinks I am a kid throwing a temper tantrum sometimes*, I laugh to myself.

A Little Tension Never Hurt Anyone

I awake the next day with a smile on my face and still in disbelief of all that's happened. I receive my, now regular, 'good morning and have a great week' text from Franklin and it certainly helps me get through my day. At lunch, my cell rings—it's him.

"Hey, beautiful. How's your day going?"

"Honestly, it's going great. I think you may have something to do with that." I say, and it's the truth. "I think this is the longest I've had a smile on my face since my father died."

"I'm glad I could help." There is a brief silence before he continues. "So, my family is coming to town next week. They're coming here for Christmas this time; they've only been here one other time. I usually go back home for the holidays."

"Oh, wow. So this is happening." I respond, feeling caught off guard.

"Oh, no. We don't *have to* do the family thing this Christmas if you don't want to, I just figured, perfect timing."

"It's not that I don't want to, but how much exactly have you told them about me or us?" I ask.

"Well, I talk about you the most to my dad. I mean, I have talked to my mom about you, but I go to my dad for advice." He chuckles. "Have you told your family about us?"

"Not at length, but they do know there is a new person in my life. We're just not as close as you and your family seem to be."

"I understand, I just want them to see the reason I've been like a different person lately."

I am a bit reserved about meeting them, but I do love this man and I will have to meet his family at some point. I also don't want to disappoint him.

"Okay," I say finally. "But just so you know, when you meet my family, it will be a totally different experience."

"I will take your word for it."

"They'll be here Christmas Eve, don't say I didn't warn you." I laugh. Checking the time, I see that my lunch hour is almost up. "Hey, love, I gotta head back in. Call you when I get home?"

"Sounds good, sweetness. Have a great rest of your day, I love you."

"Love you too." *I really do.*

The rest of my day flies by and I head home. When I arrive, I take a quick shower and get comfortable on the couch before calling Franklin. It rings a few times before he answers.

"Hey, there." He answered.

"Hey, yourself. How was your day?"

"So long. We had the longest departmental budget meeting I have ever been to and I *still* don't know why it was that long." He laughs, thinking about it.

"Oh, wow. Well, I'm glad it's over."

"Me too, babe, me too." He responds. "How'd your day go?"

"Pretty good, actually. I made a lot of progress on my project today and I am hoping it lands me this promotion I've been after."

"Oh, look at you, doing big things!" He says, excited for me.

"Here's hoping."

"Absolutely." I sense a slight hesitation in his voice.

"What's on your mind?"

"Oh, you noticed that, huh?"

"Yeah. What's up?"

"I was thinking about something you said earlier... about family."

"Oh, yeah. What part?"

"Well, it was more your reaction to meeting my family than it was anything you said."

"I know, and I'm sorry. I knew we would have to get to that point, eventually, I just didn't think it would be so soon after...you know."

"I see," he says.

I hesitated before continuing so I could carefully articulate what I wanted to say.

"Franklin, I honestly wanted us to find a since of normal before bringing our families in this, but my truest concern is that there are some things we have yet to discover about each other that I don't think would be great to discover in front of family. I didn't grow up like you."

"I understand that Cree, but I love you and you love me. I know that this is just the beginning but like you said, should fear stop us? And what do you mean, 'like me?'"

Feeling a little tension, I take a deep breath.

"I know, fear shouldn't be a hindrance, but I didn't have a well-rounded upbringing. My parents divorced when I was a teenager and remarried entirely too soon after.

It was a pretty peaceful divorce, but I chose to live with my dad and that caused a divide with my sisters that we haven't exactly settled. We just kind of let it go as we got older but lost our foundation in the process."

"So my family being tight-knit scares you?"

"No, I am just not used to that dynamic so I don't know how I would fit in it."

"Well, I can see how that would be scary." I hear what sounds like disappointment in his voice. "I haven't told them that they are meeting you yet, I just know they'll ask. I'll tell them maybe next time."

"No, Frank, don't do that. I want to meet them, I do, and Christmas is as great a time as any."

"You're sure, Credence? Because I don't want you to feel any pressure. I admit, I was a little hasty in my assumption that you would be as excited as I am."

He continues, "And you know, if you don't want to introduce me to your family yet, I am okay with that. I completely understand, and it's only fair that we move at a pace we can both keep up with. Plus, I love you." He says, more lighthearted now.

"I promise, I'm sure." I respond, "and thank you for being so understanding. I love you right back."

We continue talking about our day and plans for the week for another hour or so, then we say goodnight. I made a mental note to text Dinah in the morning, say my prayers and drifted off to sleep.

The next day, at lunch time, I get a knock on my office

door—it's the mailroom guy delivering a large bouquet of pink carnations. *Wow,* I think to myself. *I don't even remember telling him these are my favorite flowers.*

I pull out the little card that reads, *"Here is the first bouquet of, hopefully not many, apology flowers. I love you."* I smile, *how adorable.* I pick up my desk phone and call Frank to thank him for the flowers.

He answers, "Hey, sweetness, how are you?"

"I'm doing wonderful, doll. I got your apology flowers," I reply, the smile on my face even bigger now.

"Yeah, I really am sorry. Here we are at the beginning of us and I make the horrible mistake of misjudging you, *again.*"

"It's okay, Franklin. We're still getting to know each other yet and as long as we continue to communicate then we'll keep getting better at this relationship thing. Okay?"

"Okay, babe." I can sense some relief in his voice.

Our conversation goes on for a bit longer before he has to go. We made plans to have dinner this weekend to talk about what we're going to do when both our families are in town. He blows me a kiss through the phone and hangs up.

A moment later, as if she were waiting for me to get off the phone, my boss knocks on my door.

"It's open." I respond, allowing her to come in.

"So..." she says, inquiring about the flowers.

"So?" I reply, in a coy manner.

"Who's the guy that has you smiling from ear to ear?"

I chuckle, blushing. "I will confirm he is someone I am seeing but that is all you're going to get."

"Okay, okay." She responds, "I can respect that. I hope he knows how lucky he is. It looks like he already does." She touches the flowers. "They're beautiful, Cree."

"Thank you, he definitely does." She leaves my office and I finish up my work as the day moves by quickly.

After work, I take the scenic route home to visit my father. I replace the flowers that are there, adding one pink carnation from the bouquet that Frank had given me. I guess that was my symbolic way of introducing them.

"Hey daddy," I start. "I need you again. Franklin's family is coming to town for Christmas and OH!" I interrupt myself, mid-sentence. "I didn't tell you, Franklin and I are official now. We finally had the conversation I was afraid to have." I sit at my father's headstone like a little girl waiting for her father to pick her up.

"You know how I am about that." I continue. "I know, stop overthinking it, he loves me." I laugh, knowing that is what my father would say to me. I can hear his voice in my head now, *"Credence, you have a good head on your shoulders and a good man who admires and adores you. Stop doubting yourself and trust God. What does your spirit say?"*

"It says, you're right." I say out loud in response to my

own inner monologue. "I love you, daddy, and I know you'd love Franklin. I also know I have made some questionable choices in the past and you were there for those." My voice trails off, "I really wish you were here for this one."

I head home, calling Dinah on my way. She answers on the first ring, as usual. "Hey lady!"

"Hey, yourself, how's it going?"

"It goes," I state. "I just left my dad's grave. I think I talk to him more now, than I ever did…towards the end."

"You okay?" She asked.

"Yeah, I am. I actually texted you this morning because I need 'meeting the parents' advice." I say, chuckling.

"Oh goodness, are you meeting his family already?!"

"Way to make me more anxious, girl. Yes!" Laughing hard at her reaction, I continue. "He kind of sprang it on me. We got into a little tiff, he gave me apology flowers, water under the bridge."

"Wait, what?"

"Yeah, he just kind of told me that his parents are coming for Christmas and that he is going to introduce me to them. Just TOLD me. It shocked me at first because you know how I feel about my family. They don't even know I'm seeing anyone much less who."

"Right. Well I see your argument there, but good on you for saying something. And look at you, having healthy disagreements!" I laugh at her arm-chair psychology.

FROM GOD, WITH LOVE

"Yes, we did but that leaves me clueless at meeting his family. His sister I'm sure I'd be okay with seeing as I have two of those myself, but his mother is Swedish, and his father is Haitian, so they have a whole different concept of family. That tends to be one of the earliest conversations in situations like these."

"Well, how could anyone not love you."

"That's a biased opinion."

"It is, but seriously. You know that you are a genuine person and how could anyone not love you for that. That's what helped me with my hubby's parents."

"Very true, I appreciate that Di."

"I will say, though, you believe they raised a wonderful son, right? So that should tell you what type of people they are."

"You're right, and if I'm being honest, my real concern is that this was just too soon for me, I want to believe everything will go well."

"See, you didn't need my help after all."

"Girl, yes I did. This helped, more than you know."

I have been home for a little while, but I sat in my car to talk to her before going in. Once I did go in I ate some dinner, showered, and talked to God before going to bed.

"God, I cannot thank you enough, for the man that is Franklin. I've let fear of the unknown overwhelm me and that isn't who I am. I realize, now, that he is a gift from you that wasn't anything I would dare to ask for. But you knew I wouldn't ever ask because, frankly, I didn't think it was possible to have something I desired that I didn't necessarily need. You looked beyond my surface level hopes and saw my truest desire, and for that, God, I am so thankful."

    I finished up my prayers and laid down to sleep. And for the first time in what felt like forever, I was smiling.

The Meaning of Family

The rest of the week was a breeze and soon enough, it was the weekend. Franklin and I meet at what has become our usual spot—the café where we had our first date that wasn't a date. He had arrived before I did, this time, and had already picked a seat in the little reading room. As I walk up, he stands and greets me with a kiss, then sits back down.

"How was your week?"

"So good! Mostly because it flew by, though. How about yours?"

"It went well. Wrapping up the semester well, ready for a long overdue break."

"I hear that. Speaking of which, I decided to take the week of Christmas off work, you know, for the festivities." I chuckle.

He laughs in response, "You ready?"

"As I can be."

"It'll be okay, I promise. My family will love you."

"That wasn't what I was worried about, but we already had that discussion. Let's discuss what we're doing."

"Right." He lets that part of the conversation go, sensing that I didn't want to bring it up again. "So they get in town a few days before Christmas so they can go shopping. Not really for gifts, 'cause they'll bring those with them, but they love cooking and there will be one extra person this year."

"That's me." I giggle

"Yep, but I mean that is the only real plan they have—no itinerary."

"Well, they haven't been here for Christmas before, right? Maybe they can go sight-seeing."

He gives it a quick thought, "That's a good idea."

"I know, right?" I laughed. "And *maybe* I can tag along?"

"Oh, I see. Neutral environment, shopping distraction, easy to escape without seeming rude."

I laughed out loud, "See? You know me so well!"

"Okay, then dinner afterwards. Still neutral and you can still escape. Deal?"

"Deal." I lean in for a kiss. "I love you, Franklin Mathieu."

"Whoa, the whole name this time." He leans in and kisses me. "I love you right back."

The temperature is even colder now, just days before Christmas. Winter is my favorite season, and not just because of Christmas. There is just something about the cold crisp air that makes nature more beautiful—especially when the sun is high in the sky.

Franklin's parents get into town today and I am meeting them at his house before we all go out to the shopping center in Eastland tonight. I'm a little more excited than I want to admit.

I'd been off work since Friday, grateful to my boss for letting me take the time. I need all the relaxation I can get to make it, calmly, through this evening alone. I chuckle to myself at how ridiculous I am being. Just then, Frank calls.

"Hello, love. How are you?"

"Hey, sweetness, I'm doing good. I've been relaxing all day, really." I respond. "You headed to the airport, now?"

"Yeah. Is it just me or is it colder outside than it usually gets this time of year?"

"Oh, it definitely is, and I love it!" I say, excitedly, just thinking about it. "So, are you going to call me on your way back?"

"That sounds like a plan. Oh, and I did want to tell you, I guess in case it comes up." I sense his pause, but he continues, "My parents are both multilingual and they sometimes speak to each other in different languages."

"I shouldn't feel self-conscious, then?"

"Right."

"I appreciate you telling me this now, for real. Awkward is not something I want to feel tonight." It takes me a moment to realize that if both of his parents are multilingual, then he must speak more than one language too.

"Wait, so if both your parents are multilingual..."

"That makes me trilingual, my sister too. My father's native language is English, but his parents made sure he grew up speaking French and my mother taught him Swedish."

"And your mother speaks Swedish, and I assume, French too?"

"Correct."

"My goodness. I will have to have you say something to me in one of those languages one day." I smile. *Wow.*

"Anyway, my love, let me get to the airport and I'll text you when we're on our way to the house. Love you."

"Love you too, babe." We hang up and I head to my closet to lay out something to wear. As I'm sifting through my clothes, lost in thought, I realize I hadn't even gotten

Franklin a present. *Really, Cree?* I immediately calm down because I know the perfect present to go pick up for him.

Some time later, my phone buzzes. It's Frank letting me know that they are on their way back to his house. I shower, get dressed grabbing my heavier jacket, and head over to Frank's house. *Here we go.*

❦

I arrive shortly after they do so we are all getting out of our cars at the same time. I walk up as Franklin is corralling everyone in through the front door. "Hey!"

"Hey, babe!" He says, excitedly. I guess the Christmas spirit has made its way to him, too. "Perfect timing."

"I see, you need help with the luggage or anything?"

"Nah, my dad will come back out in a second. Go hang out with my mom and sister, they're just inside."

I walk in and Franklin's house looks like a page out of a Christmas catalog. His tree is tall and fully decorated, with presents already under it. There are decorations on the end tables and lights strung around the windows.

"Wow." I say, not realizing it was audible.

"I know. He loves Christmas." I turn and see this gorgeous golden curly-haired woman in a beanie, smiling at me.

"You must be Franklin's mother." I respond, smiling back.

"Anneli, so very nice to finally meet you!" she steps forward and gives me the biggest hug. "We've heard so much about you." *My word, she's a hugger. I think we're going to get along just fine.*

She releases me then steps back, giving me the most motherly once over I ever did see. Her hands reach up and cup my face. "So beautiful!" she says, sounding even more excited than she did a moment ago. I do hear her Scandinavian accent, but it isn't quite as thick as I thought it would be.

Just then, I hear another female voice, his sister, I correctly assume. "Mommy! Did she come in yet?" As she rounds the corner, she sees me standing there and is a little embarrassed. "I am so sorry."

"It's okay, I'm fairly certain I'll embarrass myself before the day is done." That seemed to ease the brief awkwardness of the situation and she gives me a hug too. "I'm Jazlyn, or just Jaz."

"Credence, or just Cree." I'm happy the introductions are over and so far they are going well. I am also a bit surprised that I am as relaxed as I am. I know I am never one to shy away from meeting new people, but I thought I'd be more nervous than this.

Not wanting to scare myself into escaping, I embrace

my calm and make conversation. "So, how was travelling? Was it as busy as they say it always is closer to Christmas?"

"Actually, it wasn't too bad." Frank's mother replies. "I think travelling during the day made the difference. Although..."

Jaz cuts her off.

"We legit almost missed our connecting flight because *someone* didn't know the gate number." They both laugh and I chuckle too.

"Well thank God, you made it." I say, genuinely happy to meet them. We're sitting in the living room, talking away before we noticed the guys haven't come in yet with luggage. I speak up. "We should see what's keeping them."

"Right." Jaz says. "I'm pretty sure they are doing the same thing we are and haven't even started taking things out of the car." *I like her. I feel a bit of my spunk in her.* "Let's go spy on them."

The three of us walk to the front door and peek through the front window shades. We laugh at how accurate Jaz's prediction was.

I break up our snickering, "Should we help them?"

"That's probably a good idea." Anneli says.

We grab our jackets and I open the front door, shouting out towards the driveway, "Y'all need anything? A hand? Some muscles?"

It was like they had forgotten us girls were in the house. Franklin's dad looks over at us, then at me and smiles.

"My word, there you are! Look at you!" He says with his thickly accented voice booming like he was using a megaphone; it scares me a little. "I'm Samuel, Franklin's father."

I smile back hoping he can't see the look of panic on my face as the closer he gets, it becomes very clear where Frank gets his height. "Here I am! So nice to finally meet you! I'm Cree." Then he, too, gives me a big bear hug. *I am going to love these people.*

We gather all of the luggage and gifts, carry them inside, and soon we are all gathered in the living room and talking. Franklin makes a pot of coffee to warm everyone up and makes me a cup of tea.

"So, Credence, what is your family doing for the holiday? Are they local?" Samuel starts.

"My mother is local, I actually grew up here. My two sisters live in other states, but they'll be down Christmas Eve."

"Oh, beautiful!" His voice carrying, he continues, "No brothers?"

"Not at all. My father was completely out-numbered." I laugh, then keep going. "My oldest sister moved to the other coast and my younger sister moved north."

"So you're in the middle?"

"Yes, sir. Right in the middle."

"Arrête de l'interroger, chérie!" Anneli speaks up, in what sounds like French.

"Je ne l'interroge pas." Samuel responds. Franklin leans over and whispers to me that his mother wants his father to stop questioning me, then he speaks up himself.

"Mom.."

"Oui mon amour?"

"English. And daddy, listen to mom. Stop questioning her." He laughs

"It's alright, Franklin. I can take it."

"See, she can take it." Samuel laughs back. We continue on like this for a while longer, then we all get ready to go shopping. Frank grabs his coat and keys and helps me with mine.

"We can all fit in my truck." he says, looking at me to make sure I was okay with that. I mouth to him that I am perfectly fine with it and as we all head to his SUV, he sneaks and gives me a kiss.

There's Something In The Air

After shopping, sight-seeing, and dinner, we go back to Frank's and relax. It was such a fun night out with his family; they are very interesting people. Jaz, being the influencer that she is, runs a successful online, self-care company that teaches women how to take intentional care of their whole selves. As much as I am into that sort of thing, I'm kind of surprised that I have never heard of nor used it.

Samuel and Anneli, both, are retired professors who now run a nursery back in Louisiana. They love doing everything together, and it is the most adorable thing I have ever seen. When one of them moves, so does the other.

Franklin turns on the fireplace in his family room, where we all ended up, then went into the kitchen for something and his mother goes with him. Jaz had stepped into another room to make a call, leaving his father and me alone.

Breaking the silence, Samuel starts talking.

"So you and my son met at church, yeah?" I feel more interrogating coming on, but I'm fine with it.

"Yes, we did. We were both new there and literally ran into each other." I smile remembering that day.

"He did tell me. So you have a relationship with God."

"Yes, sir, I do."

"What about your family?"

"We grew up going to church but honestly, I couldn't say how much He means to my sisters now." I take a moment before continuing. "We've been through a lot, this year—we lost our father."

Samuel comes over and sits next to me and grabs my hand. "I am so sorry to hear that."

"We're okay now, we grieved together as best we could, but we were never that close anyway." I trail off hoping he wouldn't ask any further. Not that he was bothering me, there just wasn't much more to tell and especially without bumming us out.

"You have a very wise and discerning spirit in you, I can feel it. You and I both know that God provides all the comfort we need. That's what matters most." I smile at him, fighting to hold back tears because as he is speaking,

FROM GOD, WITH LOVE

I hear my father's voice in his words. *Thank you daddy. And thank you for that, God.*

"Thank you, Samuel. I do know that. You just saying it gives me comfort, too." As our conversation ends, everyone starts to pile back in by the fireplace. Samuel goes back and sits next to Anneli, Franklin by me, and Jaz on the floor by the fire. The room is silent for a while, as everyone takes in the stillness of the night.

A few moments later, I check the time and let everyone know that I must be off. We stand and give our hugs and Frank walks me to my car. We stand outside in the cold, hugging for a long while, then he takes my hands.

"You okay? I heard you and my dad talking, I didn't want to listen in, but it seemed like it bummed you a little."

"Oh, no, nothing like that. Your father is a wonderful man. We got to talking about my father, but your dad really touched me with something he said." I tiptoed to kiss him goodnight. "I'm glad I came tonight, Franklin."

"Well, I'm certainly glad you did too. My family loves you, by the way. I told you." He smiles. "So do I."

"I love you too, babe. See you Christmas Eve?"

"Christmas Eve."

I leave, but instead of going home, I drive to my mother's house. I call her to let her know I'm outside and she unlocks the front door. "Well this is a surprise." She says, greeting me with a hug.

"I know but the girls will be here tomorrow night or early Christmas Eve, so I thought I'd help you get some preparations done. Plus, I was already on this side of town and didn't feel like driving all the way back home." That was closer to the truth than anything.

"Either way, glad you came." She says.

"I'm gonna hit the shower."

"Okay, I'll be watching television."

I put my bag down on the bed in my old room and hopped into the shower. After cleansing myself of the day's events and having a very long conversation with God, I get ready for bed then meet my mother in the living room.

At random, she says, "Your sister tells me you got a 'lil boyfriend." I may have lived here my whole life, but my mother hasn't, and her southern accent comes out every now and again.

Jemila. "First of all, ma, I'm in my thirties—I don't have a 'lil boyfriend'" I chuckle, "and second of all, I simply told Jemila that there was a guy I liked. Huge leap." That is literally the only thing I said to her about Frank, and that was *months* ago.

"You know how your sister is." I really do, which is why I rarely tell either of my sisters anything of substance about my life.

"Well, I'll contend with her when she gets here." I pat

my mom on the shoulder before heading off to my room.
"Shopping in the morning?"
"Sounds good, sweetie. Goodnight."
"Goodnight."

I am jarred awake the following morning to the most unholy noise. *Maya*. Why she's here a whole day early I have no idea, but I decide to get up before she storms in and annoys me to death. I quickly use the bathroom, wash my hands and face, and brush my teeth. I go back to my room and change to greet my sister.

I emerge from the safety of my room to see Maya and Jemila standing in the kitchen drinking coffee with our mother. "So, *both of you* chose to get here early."

"Yep, hey sis." Maya says.

"Hey, yourself." I reply to her, then turn to Jemila. "Hey."

"I forgot you aren't a morning person." She responds.

I completely ignore her comment and make myself a cup of tea. While that is brewing, I make some toast, butter it, and sit down to eat. "Ma, did you tell them we were going shopping today? At least that was the plan. If y'all aren't too tired from traveling, you can come, too."

"That sounds fun." Maya says—eager, I'm sure, to just

get out of the house. She loved going out for any reason anyway so I knew she wouldn't mind. Jemila, on the other hand, has a completely different personality.

"I wouldn't mind that at all." Jemila says, taking a large sip of her coffee. "Our mother told us you were still asleep, and we were going to wake you but I guess you beat us to it." She laughs.

"Actually I didn't. I heard *Maya* deep in my sleep." And with that, the heavy tension and awkwardness broke, and we are soon laughing. Sitting here around the breakfast table felt like the old us. The us that dad had to constantly separate because we did everything together. The us that loved making our parents dinner for date night because they chose to stay home and save money. The us that loved each other, once.

My mom interrupts my thinking, "So, where do you guys want to go?"

Maya chimed in, "We haven't been over to the big mall in Eastland in a while. We can get some party supplies, too, while we're out. Maybe grab lunch?"

"Party supplies?" I respond, surprised.

"Yeah, mom said she's having a party on Christmas eve." Jemila stated. *Of course mom's having a party.*

Trying not to sound too annoyed that I wasn't informed, I ask, "Okay, so this party was planned when?"

"I actually meant to tell you, but it slipped my mind." My mother responds.

"Ever the hostess." I retort.

"You know me. I only told them this morning—you were still sleeping, otherwise you would have found out at the same time as they did."

"Well, that isn't my issue. I have plans on Christmas eve. Dinah is in town so I'm going to see her and her family, and I have friends from church to exchange gifts with." Jemila gives me a glance like she knows a secret, but I dismiss her.

"That's fine, just come back by when you're finished." She tells me.

"Sweet, now let's get ready to go." I thought about the conversation I planned on having with Jemila and decided to just let it go when I recall something Samuel said to me. *You don't have to defend yourself when God's got you, Cree.*

We get to the mall with absolutely no plan on how to navigate through the other last-minute shoppers. I stop at the bookstore to get Franklin's gift and some other items and we meet back at the food court to eat.

It looks like they bought every party supply they could find, and we had a good laugh about it over our lunch. Jemila disrupts the laughter with her seriousness, as usual.

"So, who's the guy that present is for?" She says, pointing to my shopping bag.

"Why *must* you be this way?" I reply as obviously annoyed as possible.

"What way? It is for a guy, isn't it?"

"Yes, Jem, it's for a guy. He is a friend and that is all I'm telling you." She laughs at my response because she knows that I really will not tell her anything more.

"I was just wondering. Well, here's hoping it will lead to something."

"Hopefully..." I respond. I should really give her a break. I think this is her way of being the big sister she never really got to be when we were younger. "So what about you?"

She chuckles before answering, "Nothing new here. You know me, I like my life simple and men complicate things. Maya?"

"Oh, it's my turn now?" She jokes. "I have a little something going on. Too early to tell, though."

"Really?! Jemila tries to get me to cop to a secret, meanwhile you're out here in all your elusive glory?" I laugh.

We all do, which we haven't done in a while—not like this. Sometimes I miss these days and this laughter. I think we're slowly getting back to the healthy, loving space we were in before daddy died. Maybe there is something to this Christmas spirit.

A Wonderful Gift

It's Christmas Eve and I am a little anxious. There's lots for me to do today so I rose early. I wrapped all the presents I bought, leaving my family's presents in the living room, and packed the rest in my car.

I go back in to say my goodbyes to my mom and sisters. "Hey, I'll see you guys tonight, okay?"

"See you tonight." My mom responds.

I head home and do some quick cleaning before I get ready to make my rounds. It's going to be a long day but at least I get to see Dinah, who I haven't seen in the longest time, then Franklin tonight. It's still early yet so I put on a pot of tea, turn on the Hallmark channel and text Frank.

Hey, babe. What are you guys up to today?

He immediately texts back. *Hey, love! How are you? Mom and Jaz are doing some sort of yoga and dad's cooking.*

I'm doing good. Just got home from my mom's house. My sisters came a day early! SMH

Oh, no. How did that go? Good, I hope?

It did, actually. Better than I expected. I think we're heading in the right direction.

That's awesome, love.

A minute or so goes by before he sends another message.

Hey, I gotta go help my dad, but I'll see you tonight. Love you <3.

Love you, too. <3

I lay my phone down next to me and get comfortable. I have a while before Dinah gets to her parent's house, so I figure I'll watch a couple of good movies before I have to leave again. As I relax my phone buzzes again, it's Frank.

Dad says, hi!

Tell him hi, back! I chuckle to myself and watch my movies.

Soon enough, it's time to leave. I text my friends from church to make sure they're available for me to drop off their gifts and they are. After dropping off the last one, I make my way to Di's.

I ring the doorbell, a beautiful and appropriately themed chime, and she greets me at the door with a big hug.

"Bestie!"

I return the sentiment, "Bestie!" and in no time we're consumed with laughter. "Oh, my goodness I have missed you! What did you do to your hair?" She had cut it and dyed it a beautiful shade of red and it was *gorgeous*.

FROM GOD, WITH LOVE

"I've missed you too! Girl, you know I can never keep the same hair." *True.* "Come in, everyone's here."

I've known Dinah and her whole family my entire life, so I am like their adopted child. I make my way to where everyone is and give hugs all around, even to the dog.

"How is everyone?" I say to the crowd.

"We are doing great, how have you been Miss Credence?" Di's father always calls me 'Miss Credence' without fail, every time I see him.

"Doing good, sir. So good to see you again." I reply, giving him the biggest hug of them all.

Di steps in, "Okay guys, she's here to see me. Adiós!" then leads me back to the front sitting area. She has a cup of cocoa there for her and offers me some and I take her up on it.

"Where's your husband?" I ask.

"Outside with my uncles."

"In the cold? Why do guys do that? Franklin did that with his dad the day they came down from Louisiana."

"I don't know. Guys are weird." She laughs.

"The truth."

"So, tell me, how did meeting his parents go?"

"Oh it went *so* well." I tell her excitedly. I gave her every detail including my surprisingly comfortable talk with Frank's dad. "That man is something special."

"Yeah?"

"Seriously. The craziest thing about it, was that right before I went over, I had just spent time at my dad's grave, missing the talks I used to have with him. I simply said to my dad that I wished he were here for all my moments with Frank, just to guide me like he usually did.

I wasn't even praying, really, it was just something I wanted. Talking to Samuel—that's his dad's name—I felt like I was actually talking to my father."

"Oh, wow, Credence, that's beautiful."

"It really was." I smile, briefly reliving the moment.

She continues, wanting to know more about how it went. "What about his mom and sister? How do you think they like you?"

"Oh, I was worried for nothing with them. Jazlyn is his sister's name, she's just a little bit younger than us but we got along great; she even has her own successful company. And his mom, Anneli, I just the sweetest woman you'd ever meet."

"Well, they sound like a beautiful family."

"They really are. Oh, and they are all multilingual, can you believe that?" I gush. I almost love them as much as I love Franklin. *Don't get ahead of yourself, Cree.*

"Well that's cool."

"It is. They all speak three languages. Super cultured and family oriented, they are."

"That sounds amazing, Credence." She stops herself before continuing. "Before we forget...presents!"

"Oh! I have to get yours out of my car." I go out to my car, grab it and come back in.

We exchange gifts and talk for another couple of hours, as we usually do on the phone before I have to go to Franklin's house.

"Well, my darling, I must be going. I am so glad I got to see you." We stand and hug, tightly.

"Me too, friend." She replies.

I say my farewells to her family, "Merry Christmas, everyone!"

I arrive at Franklin's house just as the sun is going down; his sister answers the door. "Hey! Mom and I have been waiting all day for you to get here so we can outnumber the boys." She is going a mile a minute as she pulls me into the house and helps me with my bags and coat.

"What smells delicious in here?" I ask.

"That would be daddy's cooking." I turn and see Frank standing in the door frame with a huge smile on his face. It's like I hadn't seen him in years.

I embrace him and give him the biggest kiss, completely

forgetting that his entire family is sitting right there. "Hey." I say.

"Hey, yourself."

After speaking to everyone, I place my gifts for Frank and his family under the tree and take a seat close to the fire. Before I can ask how everyone's day went, Jaz hops in the free seat next to me. "Settle a bet for us."

"Oh, so you really meant that about girls out numbering the guys." I laugh.

"I did!" I can hear the anticipation in her voice. "Tell us, do you think *Die Hard* a Christmas movie?"

"Are you for real? Yes, *Die Hard* is a Christmas movie!" I laugh out loud. "I literally put it in my Christmas movie playlist that I watch every year!"

"I tried to tell you guys." Frank interjects.

"NO!" Jaz yells in defeat, and a little for dramatic affect. "I thought for sure you would have said it wasn't." She laughs. "We lost, mommy." Anneli laughs at the silliness.

"Oh, don't get me wrong." I say, "I love the Hallmark Christmas movies, I was watching the ones that were on earlier. But I am an eighties gal, through and through. Love me some John McClane at Christmas." I glance at Franklin, who gives me a wink.

We take to the dining room and sit down for a lovely feast. All the traditional Christmas dishes and desserts are present, including my favorite, sweet potato pie. I feel right at home sitting around this dinner table with Franklin's family but that feeling was interrupted almost immediately when Jaz usurps the conversation to talk about me and Frank.

"So, how in the world did my brother ever convince you to go out with him?"

Franklin tries to stop her but fails, "Jaz, really?"

"What? It's a legitimate question."

I laugh, buying time and semi-struggling to find the right words to say. "Well, it wasn't that hard."

"Really? You find his stuffiness attractive?" She laughs.

"Honestly? I think people underestimate him because of his meekness and completely miss the chance to get to know him." I smile at him across the table. "But it wasn't that for me. It was how he lives out his relationship with God that is most attractive to me."

Evidently satisfied with that answer, she smiles. "I'm glad my brother found someone like you—he's a lucky guy."

"Right?" I laugh in response.

Anneli chimes in at this point, "You know, people rely on God for so many things in their lives never realizing he works in these ways too."

"That's the truth." I assert.

After dinner, we settle in the living room again for some Christmas movies. When the second one is over,

Samuel gathers everyone around the Christmas tree to open presents.

"This is our tradition." Frank tells me, seeing the confused look on my face. *I was wondering*, I chuckle to myself.

"So, usually for Christmas Eve we all open at least one gift." Samuel explains, "Since it's your first Christmas with us, you pick first." He points towards a neat little stack of four beautifully wrapped presents for me and I am thoroughly surprised.

I pick up the one wrapped in pink paper since that is my favorite color. Anneli goes next, then Jaz and Franklin, then Samuel, last. As we are all talking and laughing, enjoying the moment, Frank gasps as he opens his. "Daddy."

I look over and see that it is a hand carved wall mount with their last name engraved on it. "Dad, when did you..."

"You've been down here for some time now, I think it's time you got one." Samuel, says.

"Wow, dad, thank you. I know the perfect place for it." I can see happy tears welling up in Frank's eyes as he stands up to go hang it.

Samuel follows him as Frank's mom, sister, and I start picking up the wrapping paper. As we're doing so, Anneli decides to continue the conversation we were having at dinner.

"You really do care for my son, don't you?"

"I really do."

"I agree with Jaz—I'm glad he has you. He hasn't been really successful in these things before."

"He's told me and neither have I, truthfully. And if I can be totally honest with you, I really wasn't looking for a relationship, it was one area of my life that I was completely blind to because I was holding on to so much pain and anger. I needed to wholly rely on God with Franklin and trust Him through the process."

"That's a beautiful display of faith." She puts down the scraps she's holding to cup my face. "He really has come back out of his shell since he's met you, now I see why."

We soon finish and Jaz and Anneli go into the kitchen to make coffee for everyone. I walk around Frank's house, taking in all the décor and ambiance, and I find him putting the last hook in the wall for the mount.

When it's hung, Franks goes and puts away the tools, while I stand there with his dad admiring it. After about a minute, I ask, "Did you make this yourself?"

"Yes, I did. Every man in my family has one that is always hand-made and gifted to him by his father."

"That is a lovely tradition, Samuel."

"We are a very ceremonial bunch." He laughs.

"And so very family centered. I love that about you guys." I respond and give him a hug.

"Has Franklin told you what our name means?"

"No, he has not, actually."

"It means, *'Gift of Jehovah.'*"

I am overwhelmed with emotion so quickly that I cannot stop the tears from falling. I try my best to not let Frank's dad see me, so I turn around only to find Frank coming back into the room. We make eye contact, and he sees the tears rolling down my cheeks, so he comes over to me—wrapping his arms around me.

"Hey, sweetness, are you okay?" He asks.

I step back and smile, "I am, love." *My gift from Jehovah, I absolutely am.*

What's next for Cree and Franklin? Find out from Franklin's perspective in book two.

Book II: Hope in The Tempest

I watch her as we're walking along the pier, and all I want to do is kiss her–so I do. I pulled her close to me, closing my eyes as I press my lips to hers; they're so soft and warm. She presses her arms into my chest and mine are wrapped around her. *Woman, where have you been all my life?*

"Wait," she stops me, abruptly.

"Oh, no. I'm sorry." I reply.

"No, it's not that. You didn't do anything wrong, it's just..."

"I know, you told me sex was a 'thing' for you. I didn't mean to make you feel like that's where I was going." She stares back at me, a hurt look on her face.

"Franklin, that is not at all what I said, and how did we jump to sex? And also, how dare you say that to me? I trusted you with that!" She pulls back from me and starts to walk away.

Not a smart move, Frank. "Cree, wait. Credence!" I call after her, "Please, let me explain." She stops and I catch up with her, taking a moment to collect my thoughts before I have to eat my foot again.

"I didn't mean to make it sound like you have issues or that it would be a problem for me if you did. I just meant that while I understand what sex means to you, me kissing you like that wasn't because I am turned on or anything. I didn't want that to be the reason you stopped kissing me."

The look on her face is calmer now as she replies. "Franklin, the better thing for you to do would have been to just ask me why I stopped us or what was wrong." She looks down at her feet and I can see tears welling up in her eyes.

"The reason I stopped is because *I* was getting turned on. I have enough self-control to stop before we crossed a line, but I know if I let you, *you'd* do whatever I wanted to do, even if that meant crossing a line we can't come back from."

"You're right about that, Cree. I would have kept going because it would have been what you wanted, I love you and I just want to make sure you always know it."

"I do, Frank, but what is it that *you* want? What does sex mean to you in a dating relationship?"

This really wasn't something I'd thought about, mostly because all of my relationships never included love as a caveat for sex, let alone how my beliefs played a roll. "Well, in my past relationships, it was sex just because we were together and never involved love, so this is new for me."

"Franklin," she quickly responds, "I am not your past relationships. I am your present one and it's okay to talk about the things you want in our relationship, including sex, and *without* having sex."

"Well, what if I don't know what I want as far as *our* relationship and sex?" I ask.

"That's okay too. And like I said, it's not like we need to have sex to figure it out. It is perfectly okay to wait." She smiles at me, slightly, tears gone, and grabs my hand. "Actually, I'd rather we did wait."

If I am being honest with myself, that kind of relieves me to hear she wants to wait. I know that isn't normally something guys want, but I do so that at least saves me an awkward conversation later.

Interrupting my thoughts, she says, "Come on," and grabs my hand.

"Where are we going?" I respond, puzzled.

"Somewhere less public, where we can safely and *comfortably* talk about this."

God, I love her.

CPSIA information can be obtained
at www.ICGtesting.com
Printed in the USA
LVHW091344290121
677836LV00026B/454/J